THE GREAT RACE

KEVIN O'MALLEY

Walker & Company New York

Need a funny line? I did.
So I called Dave O'Ferrall —K. O.

First published in the United States of America in June 2011
by Walker Publishing Company, Inc., a division of Bloomsbury Publishing, Inc.
www.bloomsburykids.com

For information about permission to reproduce selections from this book, write to
Permissions, Walker BFYR, 175 Fifth Avenue, New York, New York 10010

Library of Congress Cataloging-in-Publication
O'Malley, Kevin.
The great race / Kevin O'Malley.
p.   cm.
Summary: Retells the traditional tale of the tortoise and the hare as a match between the very
vain Lever Lapin and Nate Tortoise, who is tired of all of the publicity Lever's speed generates.
ISBN 978-0-8027-2158-7 (hardcover) · ISBN 978-0-8027-2159-4 (reinforced)
[1. Fables. 2. Folklore.] I. Hare and the tortoise. English. II. Title.
PZ8.2.O56Gre 2011   398.2—dc22   [E]   2010031075
ISBN 978-0-8027-2357-4 (paperback)

Art created with watercolor and FW ink on 90-lb watercolor paper
Typeset in ITC Highlander
Book design by Donna Mark

Printed in China by Toppan Leefung Printing, Ltd., Dongguan, Guangdong
2 4 6 8 10 9 7 5 3 1 (hardcover)
2 4 6 8 10 9 7 5 3 1 (reinforced)
2 4 6 8 10 9 7 5 3 1 (paperback)

Everyone was talking about Lever Lapin, the greatest runner in the world. He'd won the Dash to Dallas, the Race to Rio, and the Sprint to Spokane.

Several books were written about Lever Lapin. One was called *He's Gone*, by Otto Sight. Another was *He's on Fire*, by Stan Wellback. And of course there was the book Lever Lapin wrote about himself, *Fast Feet and Amazing Good Looks*.

Everywhere you went, people were talking about him.
And for Nate Tortoise, the whole thing was getting on his nerves.
All he wanted to do was enjoy lunch at his favorite restaurant,
La Gaganspew, and never hear the name Lever Lapin again.

But just as he was about to make slow work of his favorite dish, he overheard the ladies at the next table.

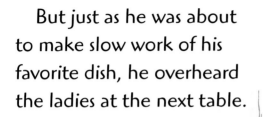

LET'S TALK ABOUT LEVER LAPIN!

"Lever has a very mysterious background," said one lady.
"I heard Lever might be a secret agent," said another lady.
"I heard Lever can walk on water," said the third lady at the table.

"Oh, brother." Nate sighed. "Can't a tortoise just enjoy a meal in peace without hearing about Lever Lapin? I mean, really, he's just a runner. I could probably even beat him in a race."

Nate must have said those last words out loud because the ladies at the table were looking at him and snickering.

At that very moment, through the door of La Gaganspew walked Lever Lapin and twenty or so personal assistants.

Nate's salad was removed. His table was given to Lever Lapin. And Nate Tortoise was moved to a table by the swinging kitchen door at the back of the restaurant.

While he ate, Lever Lapin talked to a group of reporters.
"I find myself fascinating," he said. "I am so beautiful that
when I look at myself I scream with joy. It is not easy to be me."

"Who does this hare think he is?" Nate said under his breath. "He's so dumb, if it were raining soup, he'd head outside with a fork. You know, I do believe I could beat this guy in a race."

He must have said that last line a little too loudly because the whole restaurant stopped talking and looked at him.

"What did you say?" asked Lever Lapin. "Did you say you could beat me in a race? A stubby little shell-wearer like you, beat the great Lever Lapin?"

Everyone laughed at Nate. He could feel his cheeks start to turn red but he stayed steady.

"Lapin, you're as sharp as a marble. You've got the brains of a four-year-old, and I'll bet he's glad to be rid of it. Here's what we'll do. In one week, we'll have a race. If you win, I will paint my shell with the words 'Lever Lapin is a genius.' If I win, you will wear a sign that says, 'I lost a race against a tortoise.' Do we have a deal?"

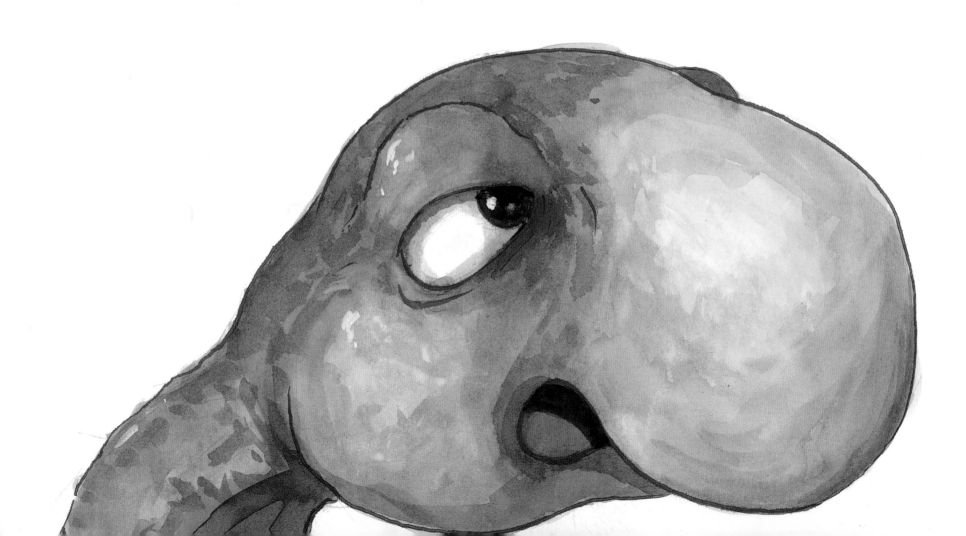

"Everyone is entitled to my opinion," said Lever Lapin. "I will race this tiny little itty-bitty tortoise and I will crush him like a marshmallow. Till next week, shell boy."

Nate went home and exercised. He did a sit-up while he watched TV. He chased after the ice-cream truck, and he ran to the pastry shop.

The whole town showed up on the day of the race.
At the starting line, Lever said, "You'd better not blink
or you won't hear me win, house-on-your-back boy."

Nate asked, "Lever, when you speak, does it echo in your head?"
With that, the starter fired his pistol and the race was on.
Lever was out of sight almost before Nate had taken a step.

"If you ran any slower, you'd be going backward," someone in the crowd yelled.
But Nate didn't give it a second thought. "See you at the finish line," he said.
And off he plodded down the road.

Lever stopped and looked back. He couldn't even see the tortoise. So he started to show off for the cheering crowds. Lever bounced really high.

He pretended to be a boxer.
He ran backward with his arms in the air.
And he yelled, "When you're as great as me, it's hard to be humble."

Lever showed off for a long time. And since the tortoise was way, way behind, he decided to take a break, have a bite to eat, and sign an autograph or two.

So when he reached La Gaganspew just before the finish line, he stopped and went inside.

La Gaganspew

Lever

Within seconds a crowd of fans stormed through the door and crushed Lever against the back wall.

OH YEAH...
I'm all that!

"Gentlemen, it's only five dollars for my autograph. And ladies, please, only one kiss for each of you. Then I really must be going. The tortoise will be here in two or three days."

Everyone laughed.

An hour later Lever was still kissing the ladies and signing autographs when the crowd outside started to cheer.

The cheering grew louder and louder.

Nate Tortoise was coming up the road.

Lever looked out the window as Nate Tortoise's head went by.

"No, wait! Get out of my way, people. Out of my way!" yelled Lever.

But he get couldn't through the crowd.
Finally, when he crawled to the finish line, it was too late.
Nate Tortoise had won the race!

The next day, Nate Tortoise quietly sat at his favorite table and slowly sipped his favorite tea as he leisurely read the newspaper headline.

"BETTER NATE THAN LEVER!" it read, and Nate said, "I couldn't agree more."